For Sammy

First published in Great Britain by HarperCollins Publishers Ltd in 1999

1 3 5 7 9 10 8 6 4 2

ISBN: 0-00-198332-6

Printed and bound in Singapore by Imago

Jungle Kids

John Wallace

Collins

An Imprint of HarperCollinsPublishers

Hi! I'm Todd – and I'm telling this story.
First, let me show you what we NORMALLY
do in the Jungle, and tell you about
the other gang members...

There are three
of us in total.

This is Jamie – the
gang's smallest member –
being messy, as usual.

And *this* is Georgina,
being bossy, as usual.

We meet every day
and go on patrol.

Sometimes
we argue...

Sometimes
we don't.

Sometimes
we fish...

Will you please
GET ON WITH
THE STORY!

Well, at about 11.30 hours, Jungle Time – that's the time
we usually have our chocolate rations – I was away from
the Jungle Hut. Suddenly a voice cried out, "EMERGENCY!
EMERGENCY! There's been an emergency!"

It was Jamie. "Something's EATEN our chocolate!" he cried.

It was THEN I noticed the footprints...
What had made them? Was it a jungle monster?
I knew one thing – this spelt
trouble for the Jungle Kids.

Todd always gets there... in the end.

Luckily, just then, I had a really, really, really good idea. Why not set a trap to CATCH this Jungle Monster?

Yes! Ha, ha! That would serve him right for stealing our chocolate. It would also give me the chance to begin an interesting scientific study into the lifecycle of this strange animal...

I'm getting off the point. Jamie had an idea for a different kind of trap. He wanted to make a giant hole, fill it with snakes, and PUSH the monster into it.

Georgina thought that sounded a little too dangerous. Her idea was to *pretend* to be nice to the monster, wait for it to come close, THEN HIT IT ON THE HEAD WITH HER KNOBKERRIE!

I thought this sounded a bit like cheating. Jungle Kids NEVER cheat.

I do.

In the end,
we decided to
hide until the
monster came...

then LEAP out
and scare him...

We decided to do it
THAT VERY EVENING...

First we got ready.

I had never been in the Jungle at night before.
I *had* to be brave.

Georgina and Jamie would *never* be frightened...

or so I thought...

We met outside at 20.15 hours, Jungle Time, as arranged. The only noise was the sound of the breeze, and Jamie...

"Do they have vampire bats in the Jungle?" he whispered.

"Only small ones," I replied.

"Shhhhhh!" whispered Georgina.

I wouldn't eat them anyway. They're too small.

Nice and crunchy, though.

The plan was to hide in the Jungle Hut.
A bar of chocolate would lure
the monster to his DOOM!

Oh, PLEASE don't let this plan work!

We huddled together. Outside, strange noises filled the night air...

I told Jamie it was just the wind.

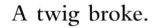

A twig broke.
I tried to keep everyone calm.

Snuffle, snuffle, SCRATCH SCRATCH.

What was THAT? IT COULD ONLY BE THE MONSTER –
COMING OUR WAY!

"Quick everybody," I yelled. **"HIDE!"**

Closer and closer it came!

WAS THIS **THE END** FOR THE JUNGLE KIDS?

Quick! Turn the page.

Aaa aaa aag gggh hhhh!

BOINK!

The Jungle Monster was A DOG! Just then he licked my face.
I knew at that moment that this dog
was a FRIENDLY dog...

WAIT! I think I'm
having an IDEA...

"If he's a friendly dog," Jamie said, "Why don't we let him JOIN OUR GANG?"

For once I agreed. He could be our GUARD DOG. He could *guard* our chocolate – instead of STEALING IT. It was the perfect solution.

Perfect solution?
You must be joking.

The next day we met up with our new gang member.
What would we call him? Discovery? Fluffy? Black Shadow?
In the end we decided on Choco.
It just seemed to fit, somehow.

Next his training.
I started with the
Jungle Rule Book.

Jamie showed him
how to climb trees,

and Georgina
bossed him around.

Choco got through his training – with FULL MARKS!
There was only one thing left to do, and that was to say,
"WELCOME TO THE GANG, CHOCO!"

"YOU'RE REALLY ONE OF US NOW!"

Now would you like to hear about my really interesting scientific experiment?
No!